for Daniel

First published in the U.S.A. 1988
by E. P. Dutton,
2 Park Avenue, New York, N.Y. 10016,
a division of NAL Penguin Inc.

Produced by Mathew Price Ltd

Printed in Hong Kong
First American Edition   OBE
ISBN: 0-525-44373-8   LC: 87-71772
10 9 8 7 6 5 4 3 2 1

Edward Loses His Teddy Bear

written by Michaela Morgan
illustrated by Sue Porter

E. P. Dutton   New York

Edward was very glad his bear had been found.
His teddy bear was pleased too.